Carrot Soup

For Emily and Josh

SIMON AND SCHUSTER

First published in Great Britain in 2006 by Simon & Schuster UK Ltd
Africa House, 64-78 Kingsway, London WC2B 6AH

Originally published in 2006 by Margaret K. McElderry Books
an imprint of Simon & Schuster Children's Publishing Division, New York

Copyright © 2006 by John Segal

A CIP catalogue record for this book is available from the British Library upon request

ISBN 1-416-91114-6

Printed in China

1 3 5 7 9 10 8 6 4 2

Carrot Soup

WRITTEN and ILLUSTRATED BY

John Segal

SIMON AND SCHUSTER

LONDON   NEW YORK   SYDNEY

It was spring – Rabbit's favourite season!

It was time to plan the garden, order
carrot seeds and look forward to enjoying his
favourite food – carrot soup.

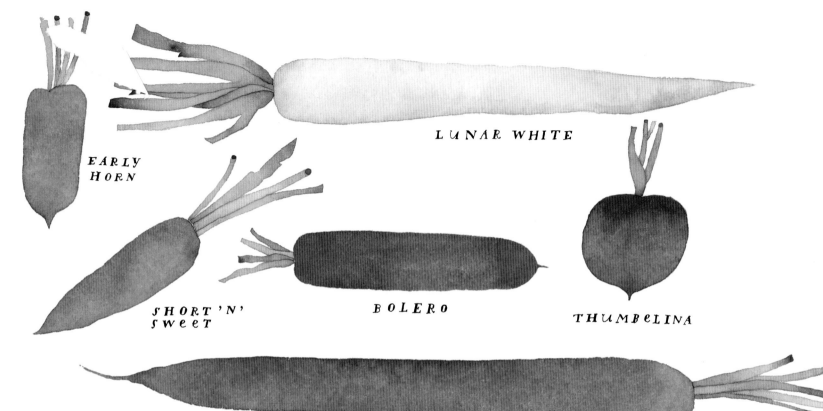

EARLY
HORN

LUNAR WHITE

SHORT 'N'
SWEET

BOLERO

THUMBELINA

SUGARSNAX

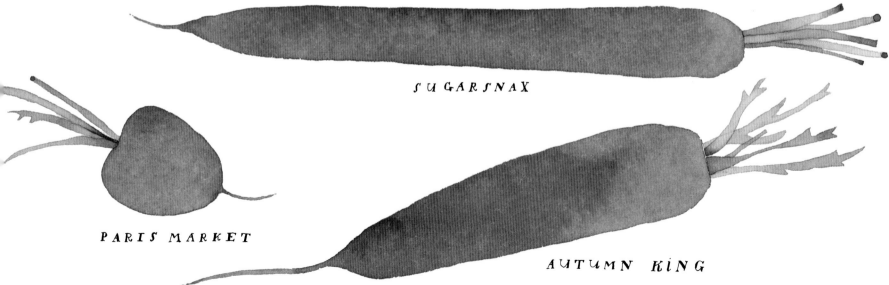

PARIS MARKET

AUTUMN KING

Rabbit ploughed

and planted.

Rabbit watered

and weeded.

He waited . . .

and waited . . .

and waited . . .

. . . until finally it was time to pick the carrots.

Rabbit gathered his tools and his wheelbarrow, and

off he went.

But something was terribly wrong at the carrot patch.

Rabbit
looked up.

Rabbit
looked down.

He looked over
and under

and inside
and out.

Rabbit saw

roots   and rocks   and dirt   and mud.

But what Rabbit did not see were . . .

. . . carrots!

There were

NO CARROTS.

They were gone!

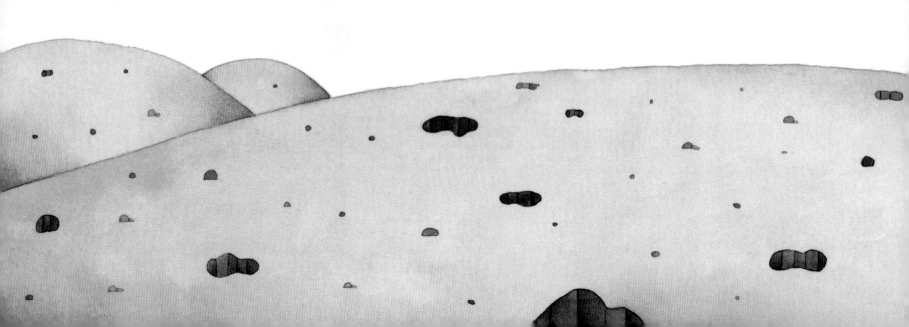

Rabbit went to see Mole.
"Mole, have you seen my
carrots?" Rabbit asked.

"Someone has stolen
my carrots!"

And Mole replied, "Rabbit, you know I don't see very well.
Why don't you ask Dog?"

"Dog, someone has taken all of my carrots!" said Rabbit.

"Have you seen them?"

"I don't care much for carrots," said Dog.
"Why don't you ask Cat?"

"Cat, I was hoping to have carrot soup tonight, but my carrots have disappeared!" said Rabbit.

"Have you seen them?"

"Carrots?" asked Cat.
"Why would I be interested in your carrots?
Perhaps Duck knows something about carrots."

Rabbit asked Duck,

"Have you
seen my
carrots?"

"I prefer fish to carrots," said Duck.

"Pig will eat anything, though. Maybe he has seen your carrots."

But Pig was nowhere to be found.

No carrot soup tonight,

thought Rabbit sadly.

Discouraged and disappointed,

Rabbit went home.

Rabbit's Favourite Carrot Soup

(Rabbit says, "Be sure to have a grown-up help you make this soup!")

1 kg carrots – washed, peeled, and shredded

4 400g cans chicken broth

2 stalks celery, chopped

1 large onion, chopped

55g butter

salt and pepper

5 sprigs fresh dill or parsley, chopped

1. Sauté the onion and celery in butter in a large covered pot until tender. Add the shredded carrots and chicken broth. Bring to the boil.

2. Reduce heat and simmer with the pot covered for about 30 minutes.

3. Let cool slightly. Puree the mixture in a blender or food processor until smooth.

4. Add salt and pepper to taste. Add dill or parsley. Serve.

Delicious!

Serves 10 (or one very hungry Rabbit).